To Baby Heller,
Have fun with your
Raggedy Ann & Andy Dolls
and enjoy reading this story
book Love
Aunt Jenny

MY FIRST
Raggedy

Ann

Raggedy Ann

and

Rags

ADAPTED FROM THE STORIES BY

JOHNNY GRUELLE

ILLUSTRATED BY JAN PALMER

SIMON & SCHUSTER BOOKS FOR YOUNG READERS

NEW YORK   LONDON   TORONTO   SYDNEY   SINGAPORE

SIMON & SCHUSTER BOOKS FOR YOUNG READERS

 An imprint of Simon & Schuster Children's Publishing Division

1230 Avenue of the Americas, New York, New York 10020

The text of this book is set in Jenson.

The illustrations are rendered in watercolor and ink.

Printed in Hong Kong

10 9 8 7 6 5 4 3 2 1

Library of Congress Cataloging-in-Publication Data
My First Raggedy Ann: Raggedy Ann and Rags: adapted from stories by Johnny Gruelle /
illustrated by Jan Palmer.
p. cm.
Summary: After joining Raggedy Ann and Andy in Marcella's household, a frisky puppy
appropriately called Rags helps rescue Ann when she goes sailing one day.
ISBN 0-689-82977-9 (hc)
[1. Dolls—Fiction. 2. Dogs—Fiction.] I. Gruelle, Johnny 1880?–1938.
Raggedy Ann and Rags. II. Palmer, Jan, ill.
PZ7.M9764 2000
[E]—dc21
99-32227
CIP

The History of Raggedy Ann

One day, a little girl named Marcella discovered an old rag doll in her attic.
Because Marcella was often ill and had to spend much of her time at home,
her father, a writer named Johnny Gruelle, looked for ways to keep her entertained.
He was inspired by Marcella's rag doll, which had bright shoe-button eyes and
red yarn hair. The doll became known as Raggedy Ann.

Knowing how much Marcella adored Raggedy Ann, Johnny Gruelle wrote
stories about the doll. He later collected the stories he had written for Marcella and
published them in a series of books. He gave Raggedy Ann a brother, Raggedy Andy,
and over the years the two rag dolls acquired many friends.

Raggedy Ann has been an important part of Americana for more than half a century,
as well as a treasured friend to many generations of readers. After all, she is much more
than a rag doll—she is a symbol of caring and love, of compassion and generosity.
Her magical world is one that promises to delight
children of all ages for years to come.

One clear, summer night, Raggedy Ann, Raggedy Andy, and Uncle Clem were sitting in front of the playhouse. Marcella had played outside with them that afternoon, and had been called into the house. Now the sun had gone down, and the evening shadows had turned everything a lovely purple. The little fireflies came up out of the grass and sailed high into the air.

"Who knows?" Raggedy Ann said in a whispery, cotton-soft voice. "Perhaps we may see the fairies."

"Oh! I wish we could," said Uncle Clem.

"*Shh!*" said Raggedy Andy very quietly. "What is that?" They heard something like a twig snapping near the orchard fence. The dolls waited.

The moon had risen, and now a tiny puppy dog came into sight. The puppy's fur was white with brown spots, and he had soft, black eyes. He trotted up to the dolls and sniffed each of them in turn.

"You are very small to be on your own at night," Raggedy Ann told the dog. "Where is your mama?"

The tiny puppy dog said nothing. He licked Raggedy Ann's face with his pink tongue, climbed into her lap and turned around, and fell asleep. Raggedy Ann and the other dolls sat quietly, watching the night and the fireflies and the puppy dog.

Bright and early the next morning, Marcella ran out to the playhouse.
When she saw the dolls, she ran back to the house. "Daddy! Mama!
Come quick!" she cried.

Mama and Daddy followed Marcella to where the dolls sat. Raggedy
Ann held a tiny puppy dog on her lap, partly covered by her apron.

"Maybe the fairies brought him," Marcella said.

"I wonder where his mother is," said her daddy. "Well, we can't leave
him out here."

Carefully, Marcella picked up the puppy dog and brought him into the kitchen. Her daddy followed with the dolls. Mama found a saucer of warm milk for the puppy, and he lapped it up hungrily.

"What are you going to call him?" Daddy asked.

"Raggedy Ann found him," Marcella said. "I shall call him Rags."

All that summer, Rags drank warm milk, and he grew bigger and stronger. He learned to bark, though he could never tell the dolls where he came from or who his mama was.

Marcella liked to dress Rags in a doll's cap and nightie. She fed him treats, and sometimes they played tug-of-war with an old stocking. Rags chewed Papa's socks until Mama found out and said, "Bad dog!" so sternly that Rags went to hide in the closet.

But he couldn't be downhearted, especially after one of Marcella's tea parties, when he would lick the crumbs from the dolls' faces. Every night at bedtime, Daddy would let Rags outside, and he would run around the house and bark. Then he would fall asleep in the garden, keeping one eye half-open for the rabbits.

Most nights, Marcella put the dolls to sleep in the nursery, but if she was called to an early supper, the dolls would stay outside. One evening in August, some of them were left on the beach. As soon as he was let outside, Rags ran around the house. He barked at the playhouse and at the stone wall by the beach. Then he joined the dolls near the water, where he barked and barked at the moon, wagging his stumpy tail.

"Mercy!" said Raggedy Ann. "What are you barking at?"
Rags said nothing, but trotted up to Raggedy Ann and licked her hand. She had to laugh, for she knew he just wanted to pretend he was taking good care of them all.

"Raggedy Ann, will you come sailing with me?" asked Squeakie. She was a new doll in the nursery, stuffed with wood and sawdust. She had found a flat board just the size for the two dolls, with a string tied to the front.

Raggedy Ann thought a sail was a fine idea, so she and Squeakie pushed the wood into the water and climbed on top. Gentle waves lapped at the board, and a sudden breeze pushed them away from the shore, where Raggedy Andy, Uncle Clem, and Cleety the clown were looking for hermit crabs, and Rags was barking at minnows in the shallow pools.

Raggedy Ann and Squeakie sat, arms around each other, looking at the silvery trail of the moon on the water. It was so peaceful, they didn't realize how far they had drifted, and none of their friends onshore noticed their absence. Not even Rags noticed, and he made it his business to notice everything!

"Goodness! What a noise!" Raggedy Andy exclaimed. Rags was barking furiously, running up and down at the edge of the water.

"Look!" Cleety said, pointing. "Raggedy Ann and Squeakie have gone sailing."

"They're awfully far out," said Uncle Clem. "Perhaps they need to be rescued."

"But how?" asked Raggedy Andy. "We can't swim, for our stuffing will be waterlogged if we try. No, Rags," he added, for Rags had flung himself into the water as if prepared to swim all the way out to the two sailors.

"I know!" Cleety said suddenly. "The steamboat. It runs very fast in the water."

Marcella had a little steamboat that she often brought down to the water, which ran by a little key that turned a paddle wheel. It lay not far away on the beach.

They all ran over to the steamboat and carried it to the water. But when they tried to climb on board, the little boat turned over and sank.

"This will never do," said Uncle Clem. "All of us except Cleety are too large to ride on the steamboat. Cleety will have to be engineer and captain and everything."

So Cleety the clown climbed onto the little steamboat, and Raggedy Andy and Uncle Clem waded out into the water and gave it a grand push. Rags barked and dashed into the water and back again, but Raggedy Andy took hold of his collar before he could plunge into deep water and swim alongside the boat. Cleety wound the key in the smokestack, and then he waved to his friends and guided the steamboat across the water.

Raggedy Andy and Uncle Clem and Rags walked back to the stone wall and sat down. The two dolls and the puppy watched as Cleety and the steamboat sped away across the silvery wake of the moon. Rags looked up at Raggedy Andy from time to time, as if to say, "I can swim out and help Cleety," but he kept still and didn't bark.

Cleety wound and wound the key, and the steamboat sailed through
the water. A wild duck swooped down and was so startled by the sight of
a clown on a little boat that it flew away, not even answering Cleety's
question: "Have you seen two nice dolls drifting on a board?"

So Cleety sailed on and on.

Cleety circled around the bunches of swamp grass toward Peach Island. He had just about given up hope of finding the dolls when he heard Squeakie's voice, from far across the water, say, "What is that thing sailing out there, Raggedy Ann? It looks like a tiny ship."

Then Raggedy Ann said, "It *is* a tiny ship, Squeakie, and look! Cleety the clown is making it go."

So Cleety ran the little steamboat up to where Raggedy Ann sat upon the wooden board, holding Squeakie on her lap.

"My goodness!" said Raggedy Ann. "How glad we are to see you, Cleety. We have had a most delightful sail, but it would never do for us to drift out to sea."

"That's why I'm here," Cleety said. "Raggedy Andy and Uncle Clem and Rags would have come, but the little steamboat wouldn't hold them."

"Then we shall have to hug them when we are back onshore," said Squeakie. "And I intend to hug you, too!"

Cleety thought that would be very nice, and said so. Then he tied the board to the little steamboat, turned the key, and headed for shore.

The journey back was a slow one, for Raggedy Ann and Squeakie and the board were a heavy cargo, and Cleety had to rewind the key many times. As they neared the beach, they heard loud barking. Rags had spotted them, and he was running excitedly up and down at the edge of the water.

"Look!" said Raggedy Andy. He also had spotted the little steamboat and the two dolls on the board. He and Uncle Clem joined Rags by the water.

Rags couldn't wait another second. He jumped into the water and swam out to meet the sailors, almost upsetting the little steamboat with the waves he made.

"Now, Rags, please be careful," Raggedy Ann said. "We are glad to see you, but you must not sink us!"

So Rags swam behind the little steamboat and carefully placed his black nose against the board. He pushed the board and the steamboat toward the beach until Raggedy Andy and Uncle Clem could pull them the rest of the way.

Once onshore, Raggedy Ann and Squeakie gave Cleety big hugs for rescuing them, and then they hugged Raggedy Andy and Uncle Clem for good measure.

Rags ran around them in circles. He was so happy to see everyone back safe and sound! Then he shook himself all over.

"Stop, Rags," said Raggedy Ann. But she wasn't really angry. She sat, and Rags flopped down beside her. The other dolls sat in the sand nearby, and that was how Marcella found them in the morning.

"Oh, poor babies. You're all damp!" Marcella said. She gathered the dolls in her arms. "I must take you inside and feed you breakfast, or you will surely catch a chill." Raggedy Ann looked at Raggedy Andy, and their shoe-button eyes twinkled.

As for Rags, he ran around the house three times and then went to sleep in the garden, with one eye half-open for the rabbits.